MARC BROWN

Arthur Loses His Patience

D0518293

D.W. was driving Arthur crazy.

She was playing her Crazy Bus tape
over and over.

"Can't you listen to a different tape?" asked Arthur.

"This is my favorite," said D.W. "Besides, it helps me do my work."

"What work?" asked Arthur.

"I'm making a shoebox scene for Mom and Dad's anniversary," D.W. explained.

"A diorama," said Arthur.

"Yes," D.W. said, turning up the volume on her tape player. "I'll stop playing Crazy Bus as soon as I finish."

Arthur looked down at the mess.

"You're not anywhere near finished," he said.

"I guess I'll be playing my Crazy Bus tape
for a while," said D.W.

"Okay, okay!" said Arthur. "I'll help you."

"You will?" asked D.W.

"I'll do anything to stop that tape," said Arthur.

"First we have to color the outside of the box," said D.W.
"I like pink...but Dad likes yellow...and blue is Mom's favorite..."

"How about green?" said Arthur.

"Well..." D.W. hesitated.

But Arthur was already coloring as fast as he could color.

"It's not right," said D.W.

"It's fine," said Arthur.

"It has to be perfect," said D.W. She added some spots.

"It needs beads or feathers," said D.W.

Arthur looked at his watch.

"Beads or feathers?" asked D.W.

"Feathers," said Arthur.

"I'll use beads," said D.W. "Now...where are they?"

Arthur tapped his fingers impatiently to the Crazy Bus song.

"I found my beads!" shouted D.W.

"Watch carefully," said D.W. "The beads all have to face the same way."

She glued one bead onto the box.

"This way is faster," said Arthur, grabbing a big handful.

"That looks terrible," said D.W.

Arthur looked at his watch again.

"Bionic Bunny is on!" said Arthur. "I've got to go."

"But you said you would help me," said D.W.

"I'll help you tomorrow!" he shouted.

The next day, Arthur heard the Crazy Bus tape.

"Not again," he groaned.

"Arthur, can you help me now?" called D.W.

"Sorry," Arthur said. "I have to meet Buster at the Sugar Bowl."

The next morning, D.W. found Arthur right after breakfast.

"Arthur, I really need..." began D.W.

"I'm in a hurry," said Arthur. "Big game today. See you later, D.W."

Two nights later, Arthur heard sniffling and the Crazy Bus song coming from D.W.'s room.

"What's wrong?" asked Arthur.

D.W.'s eyes filled with tears.

"My present won't be ready in time," she said.

Arthur looked inside the shoebox.

"It's a Cloud Kingdom," said D.W. "With a glittery rainbow...and two unicorns."

"But my unicorns don't look like unicorns," she said.

"These aren't so bad," said Arthur.

Arthur trimmed the two unicorns a little.

D.W. stopped sniffling and started coloring.

Arthur added a little more glue to the feathers, and they started to look like clouds.

"The rainbow goes over there," said D.W.

"Okay," said Arthur.

When D.W. played her Crazy Bus tape louder, Arthur wanted to complain. But he didn't.

Arthur started to hum along.

"I think it's finished," said D.W.

She looked at Arthur and started to laugh.

"You look funny," she said.

"So do you," laughed Arthur.

In the morning, D.W. gave Mom and Dad her present.

"Wow!" said Dad.

"It's wonderful," said Mom. "Did you do this all by yourself?"

"Not exactly," said D.W. "Arthur helped a little."

"And Crazy Bus helped a lot!" said Arthur.